THE BOXCAR CHILDREN®

THE LIGHTHOUSE MYSTERY

Time to Read® is an early reader program designed to guide children to literacy success regardless of age or grade level. The program's three levels correspond to stages of reading readiness, making book selection straightforward, and assuring that when it's time for a child to read, the right book is waiting.

— Level — 1	Beginning to Read	• Large, simple type • Basic vocabulary	• Word repetition • Strong illustration support
— Level — 2	Reading with Help	• Short sentences • Engaging stories	• Simple dialogue • Illustration support
— Level — 3	Reading Independently	• Longer sentences • Harder words	• Short paragraphs • Increased story complexity

Library of Congress Cataloging-in-Publication data is on file with the publisher.

Copyright © 2020 by Albert Whitman & Company
First published in the United States of America
in 2020 by Albert Whitman & Company
ISBN 978-0-8075-4548-5 (hardcover)
ISBN 978-0-8075-4549-2 (ebook)

THE BOXCAR CHILDREN® is a registered trademark
of Albert Whitman & Company.

TIME TO READ® is a registered trademark
of Albert Whitman & Company.

Printed in China
10 9 8 7 6 5 4 3 2 1 HH 24 23 22 21 20

Cover and interior art by Shane Clester

Visit the Boxcar Children® online at www.boxcarchildren.com.
For more information about Albert Whitman & Company,
visit our website at www.albertwhitman.com.

THE BOXCAR CHILDREN®

THE LIGHTHOUSE MYSTERY

Based on the book by
Gertrude Chandler Warner

Albert Whitman & Company
Chicago, Illinois

"Can we stop soon?"
said Benny Alden.
"I'm hungry."
The Aldens were driving
home from Aunt Jane's.
"If we stop each time you get
hungry, we'll never get home!"
said Violet.
Grandfather laughed.
"That's all right," he said.
"We will stop in Conley.
We can picnic by
the old lighthouse!"

"Can we go to the top
of the lighthouse?"
Benny asked at Hall's Grocery.
"You can do more than that,"
Mr. Hall said.
"You can stay there!
We do not use it anymore.
We rent it to visitors."
If one thing made Benny
forget about being hungry,
it was an adventure.
"Can we stay, please?"
Benny said.
Grandfather smiled.
"A few nights wouldn't hurt."

Henry, Jessie, Violet, and Benny
loved to explore new places.
At one time, the children
had lived in a boxcar.
They had many adventures
in the boxcar.
Then Grandfather found them.

Now they had a real home.
And they still had all kinds
of adventures!

"This will be your room,
Grandfather," Benny said.
He ran up the circle staircase.
"Henry's room!" he called.
Benny ran up again.
"Jessie and Watch!"
Benny ran up once more.
This time, he was out of breath.
"Violet...and...Benny!"
he called.
The children laughed.
They wondered what surprises
their funny new home
might hold.

The Aldens' first surprise
was a loud one.
In the middle of the night,
Watch began to growl.
He barked and howled!

The children could not find
why Watch was upset.
At last Benny said,
"I think I smell food."
Violet giggled.
"You must still be dreaming."
The Aldens went back to bed.

In the morning, the children
went exploring.
They passed by a little shack
and went down to the beach.
Violet found all kinds of shells.
Benny found strange seaweed.

But what Henry found
was extra-strange.
It was full of shapes and scribbles.
"I can't make sense of this paper,"
Henry said.
"Maybe it's a clue!" said Benny.

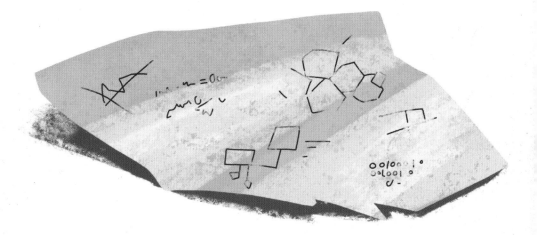

For supper, the Aldens planned
a cookout on the beach.
On the way to Hall's Grocery,
they saw a young man.
He looked very tired
and not very friendly.

The children asked Mr. Hall
about the young man.
"That is Larry Cook,"
said Mr. Hall.
"He's a nice boy.
But he's been upset lately."
Why was the young man
in such a bad mood?

On the beach, the Aldens made
chairs out of rocks and sand.
Grandfather cooked hot dogs
over the fire.
Benny cooked a piece
of seaweed on a stick.
"It's seafood!" he said.

But when Benny took a bite,
all he tasted was salt.
He gave the rest to Watch.

After supper, the children sat
on top of the lighthouse.
They watched the stars
over the sea.
One star kept moving.
It was not a star at all.
"It's a boat!" said Henry.
"How strange," Jessie said.
"Who could be out at this hour?"

Later that night, Watch again began to bark and howl. This time, the children found a clue out the window.

Someone was on the beach!
The person went from
the dock to the empty little
shack next-door.

In the morning, the Aldens
looked for more clues.
The little shack was locked.
Henry helped Benny peek in.

"I see books," said Benny.
"And paper, like Henry found.
And a stove and a frying pan!"
Benny jumped down.
"I knew I smelled food
at night!"
But what did it mean?

At the dock, Larry Cook
was working with his father.
Larry looked even more tired
and upset than before.

The name on the boat
gave Violet an idea.
Was the boat the light they
saw at night?

SEA STAR

At the store, Mr. Hall asked, "Are you children coming to the Village Meal tomorrow?" He said the meal was to raise money to help others. "Who makes the meal?" said Jessie.

"Larry Cook," said Mr. Hall.

"Larry?" said Benny.

"We thought he was mean!"

Mr. Hall sighed.

"I think he is just sad.

His friends went off to school.

Larry stayed to help his father."

The Aldens knew just what to do. This time when they passed the *Sea Star*, Benny blurted, "Do you want a friend?"

Larry did not know what to say.
"I think he means…"
Jessie said.
"Do you want help with
the Village Meal?"
For the first time, Larry
gave a small smile.

SEA STA

The next morning, the children
helped Larry make the meal.
The recipe was full of shapes
and scribbles.
Henry could not understand it.
But Larry read it easily.

When the cooking was done, the children tried their chowder. "Your seafood is much better than mine," said Benny.

The meal was a big success.
Still, Larry did not seem happy.

"You are a gifted cook,"
a woman told Larry.
"Do you study at school?"
But the woman could tell
by Larry's frown that
the answer was no.
"I think Larry wants to go
to school like his friends,"
Benny whispered.

That night it rained
and stormed.
The children talked about
Larry and the boat on the sea
and the little shack next-door.
"Maybe Larry takes the
Sea Star out at night,"
said Violet.
"That is why he is so tired."
"I think those are his
recipes in the little shack,"
said Henry.

Jessie spoke up.
"He must go out fishing
and then practice cooking!"
"That's why his food
is so tasty!" said Benny.

The children looked outside.
There was only one star out.
It was moving all around.
Larry was out in the storm!
He needed their help!

The children took their
flashlights to the top
of the lighthouse.
They shined their lights
at the mirror.
"It's working!" said Benny.
Slowly, the *Sea Star* followed
the light in.

Larry was cold and wet,
but he was safe.
Larry told his father
what had happened.
He thought his father
would be mad.

But Mr. Cook apologized.
"I did not know you
wanted to cook so badly.
I should have let you
go off to school."

The next day, a visitor arrived.
It was the woman from
the Village Meal.
She had heard Larry's story.
"How would you like to study
to be a chef?" she asked.
Larry looked at his father.
Mr. Cook nodded.

"Hooray!" Benny said.
"You won't have to cook
in the night!"
Larry gave his biggest smile yet.
Benny was right.
For the first time…

his future was
looking bright.

Keep reading with the Boxcar Children!

Henry, Jessie, Violet, and Benny used to live in a Boxcar. Now they have adventures everywhere they go! Adapted from the beloved chapter book series, these early readers allow kids to begin reading with the stories that started it all.

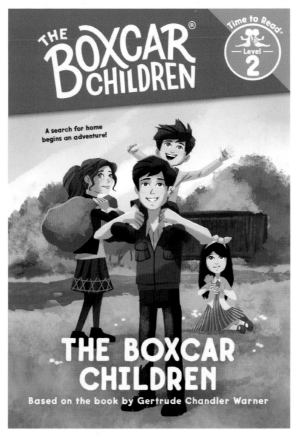

HC 978-0-8075-0839-8 · US $12.99
PB 978-0-8075-0835-0 · US $3.99

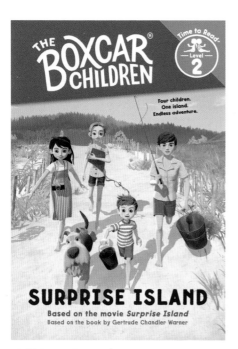

HC 978-0-8075-7675-5 · US $12.99
PB 978-0-8075-7679-3 · US $3.99

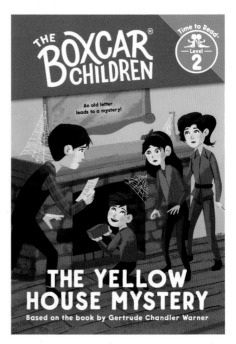

HC 978-0-8075-9367-7 · US $12.99
PB 978-0-8075-9370-7 · US $3.99

HC 978-0-8075-5402-9 · US $12.99
PB 978-0-8075-5435-7 · US $3.99

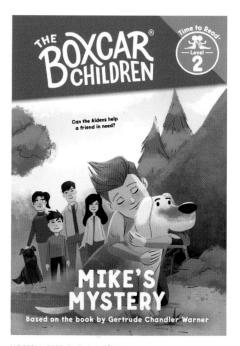

Can the Aldens help
a friend in need?

MIKE'S MYSTERY

Based on the book by Gertrude Chandler Warner

HC 978-0-8075-5142-4 · US $12.99
PB 978-0-8075-5139-4 · US $3.99

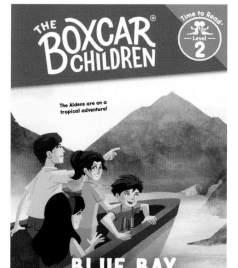

The Aldens are on a
tropical adventure!

BLUE BAY MYSTERY

Based on the book by Gertrude Chandler Warner

HC 978-0-8075-0795-7 · US $12.99
PB 978-0-8075-0800-8 · US $3.99

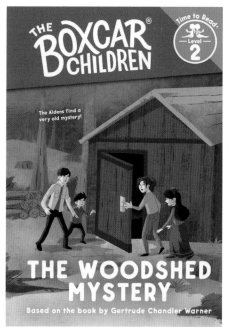

The Aldens find a
very old mystery!

THE WOODSHED MYSTERY

Based on the book by Gertrude Chandler Warner

HC 978-0-8075-9210-6 · US $12.99
PB 978-0-8075-9216-8 · US $3.99

GERTRUDE CHANDLER WARNER discovered when she was teaching that many readers who like an exciting story could find no books that were both easy and fun to read. She decided to try to meet this need, and her first book, *The Boxcar Children*, quickly proved she had succeeded.

Miss Warner drew on her own experiences to write the mystery. As a child she spent hours watching trains go by on the tracks opposite her family home. She often dreamed about what it would be like to set up housekeeping in a caboose or freight car—the situation the Alden children find themselves in.

While the mystery element is central to each of Miss Warner's books, she never thought of them as strictly juvenile mysteries. She liked to stress the Aldens' independence and resourcefulness and their solid New England devotion to using up and making do. The Aldens go about most of their adventures with as little adult supervision as possible— something else that delights young readers.

Miss Warner lived in Putnam, Connecticut, until her death in 1979. During her lifetime, she received hundreds of letters from girls and boys telling her how much they liked her books.